Dear Parent:
Your child's love of r

Every child learns to read in a d............ own
speed. Some go back and forth between reading .... ad
favorite books again and again. Others read through each level in
order. You can help your young reader improve and become more
confident by encouraging his or her own interests and abilities. From
books your child reads with you to the first books he or she reads
alone, there are I Can Read Books for every stage of reading:

SHARED READING
Basic language, word repetition, and whimsical illustrations,
ideal for sharing with your emergent reader

BEGINNING READING
Short sentences, familiar words, and simple concepts
for children eager to read on their own

READING WITH HELP
Engaging stories, longer sentences, and language play
for developing readers

READING ALONE
Complex plots, challenging vocabulary, and high-interest topics
for the independent reader

I Can Read Books have introduced children to the joy of reading
since 1957. Featuring award-winning authors and illustrators and a
fabulous cast of beloved characters, I Can Read Books set the
standard for beginning readers.

A lifetime of discovery begins with the magical words **"I Can Read!"**

Visit www.icanread.com for information
on enriching your child's reading experience.

Super Wings: A Super First Day
Copyright © 2019 FUNNYFLUX / ALPHA
All rights reserved. Printed in the United States of America.
www.icanread.com

ISBN 978-0-06-290720-2

19 20 21 22 23   LSCC   10 9 8 7 6 5 4 3 2 1   ❖   First Edition

A SUPER FIRST DAY

Adapted by Steve Foxe
Based on the episode "Backpack
for Baraka" by Dale Schott

HARPER
An Imprint of HarperCollinsPublishers

I am Jett.

Sometimes I'm a plane.

Sometimes I'm a robot.

I take boxes across the world.
This box is going to Kenya.

It's the first day of school
for a little boy in Kenya.
But his backpack has a hole!

"I'm Jett!" I say.

"I'm on time, every time.
This box is for you."

"Thanks, Jett!" the boy says.
"Now let's go to school!"

We walk to school.
We see many animals.

"Look!" I say.

"That giraffe is stuck!"

We work together.

We help save the giraffe.

Great work!

Plop! Plop!

Oh no!

It starts to rain.

18

The river starts to flood.

"We are stuck!" the boy says.

"We need to save
the animals.
And I need to get to school!"

I call Donnie and his friends.

They come to save the day.

I know!

We can make a boat.

All aboard!

"We did it!" the boy says.
"We saved the animals.
But now I'm late for school!"

"Don't worry," I say.

"This can be a speedboat!"

"It's working!" the boy says.

"But we are going too fast!"

Remi comes to the rescue!

She uses her hook.

She catches us just in time.

The boy makes it to school.

"Bye!" the boy says.

"Thank you, Super Wings!